THE CAT WHISPERER

JEFF GOTTESFELD

SADDLEBACK
EDUCATIONAL PUBLISHING

red rhino
b OO k s®

With more titles on the way ...

SADDLEBACK
EDUCATIONAL PUBLISHING
www.sdlback.com

ISBN-13: 978-1-62250-955-3
ISBN-10: 1-62250-955-2
eBook: 978-1-63078-178-1

Printed in Guangzhou, China
NOR/0715/CA21501107

19 18 17 16 15   1 2 3 4 5

MEET THE

Jen

Age: 12

Family Heritage: her great-grandfather was from French Cameroon

Favorite Movie: *Mean Girls*

Lifelong Dream: to trace her family tree

Best Quality: always bounces back, resilient

CHARACTERS

Age: 4 human years; 33 cat years

Best Time of Day: midnight, when everyone is sleeping

Favorite Food: chocolate chip cookies

Biggest Fear: canned cat food

Best Quality: knows herself completely

1
WORST CAT EVER

The cat stared at Jen. Her name was Mimi. Mimi was a bad cat. Still, Jen offered Mimi her hand.

"Come on," Jen urged. "Be cool, like Dawn's cat. Or sweet, like the cat down the street. Or even funny, like some cats on YouTube."

Mimi kept staring. She was black with white paws. Her tail was bushy. Her ears were small. Her eyes were the color of grass.

Jen sighed. Two years ago her family adopted Mimi. It was right after they came to California. It had been Jen's idea. She'd seen an ad in a coffee house: FREE TO A GOOD HOME! GREAT CAT!

There had been a picture of Mimi too. She looked nice. All Jen's new friends had pets. But not Jen.

Jen picked a good time to ask her mom and dad. Her dad had a new job near Los

Angeles. Her parents wanted Jen to be happy in their new home.

Jen was fine with the move. She loved the sunny days. She didn't even mind the little earthquake the first week they were there. The house shook for a few seconds. It had been fun.

She went to Mimi and picked her up. The cat gave a cry.

Meow

"How about if I took you to school?" Jen

asked. "Maybe that would make you a nice cat. Don't you want to be in sixth grade?"

The cat cried again. Louder. Then she hissed.

"Fine! Go be evil. I don't care anymore."

Devil Kitty?

Jen put Mimi down. The cat jumped to Jen's bed. Then to her desk. And then, in a huge leap, to the top of her closet. There was a shelf up there. She hissed again.

Oh no! Jen shook her head so hard her brown curls danced. All her good stuff was on that shelf. Her photos. Her writing. Mimi might claw it. Or drool on it. Or do even worse to it. That's how bad she was. Jen was sorry they ever brought her home.

She had to get Mimi down, so she stood on a chair. "Come on, Mimi. Help me out. Get down. Oh! Wait. I know."

There were cat treats in the kitchen. Jen ran and got them. Then she came back to her room. Mimi was still on the closet shelf. She stared at Jen with scorn.

Jen got on the chair. She held a treat in her hand. "Here you go, Mimi," she called in a soft voice. "Owww!" Jen yanked her hand back. The cat had scratched her. There were three long red lines on her arm. "That hurt!"

Mimi didn't seem to care. She just jumped down, landing on all four feet. Then she hissed again and walked away.

Jen gritted her teeth. Mimi was not just a bad cat. She was the worst cat ever.

2
BAD DREAM

"Morning."

Jen kept her eyes closed. It was the weekend. Too early to be awake. She didn't even know who was in her room. She didn't care.

"Morning. Please go away," she said.

Her friend Dawn came over last night. They watched a movie and played cards. Then Dawn went home.

Hmmm …

Go fish!

Jen's arm hurt. A lot. So much she took some medicine before bed. That darn cat.

COD LIVER OIL

← grandma's remedy

"Sorry about your arm."

Ah. Female voice. Her mom. But it didn't sound like her mom. Maybe her mom had a cold.

"Lemme sleep, Mom."

Jen pulled a pillow over her head.

"I said, 'Sorry about your arm!' I'm not going to leave you alone. Why don't you say anything? Don't be so darn rude, Jennifer."

Whoa. Her mom didn't speak that way.

And her mom only ever called her Jen. Never her full name. Jen moved the pillow to see who was there.

No one was there. Just Mimi. The cat was on the floor near her bed.

"Go away, Mimi," Jen told the cat. "I'm not your fan."

"I said I was sorry," the cat said.

Jen stared at Mimi. The cat had just

talked to her. But that couldn't be. Cats didn't talk. She hadn't even heard Mimi's meow. But she'd heard words in her head.

No. No way.

Jen touched her own head to see if she had a fever. Nope. Cool as a cuke. She decided she was dreaming.

"I'm going back to sleep," she told the cat.

Mimi shrugged. "Do what you want. I just wanted to say sorry. By the way, if you let me outside, I'd be a lot happier. And those treats? The worst. Did you ever try one? No? I didn't think so. They taste like wood chips. Better treats. Better treatment. Better cat. Do the math."

Jen's eyes got wide. Her heart beat faster. There was no doubt about it. Her cat was talking to her.

How could that be?

She decided again that she was dreaming.

"Go away, Mimi," she told the cat. "Get out of my dream."

Mimi didn't move. Jen tossed a pillow at the cat in her dream. Mimi ran away.

3
NO DREAM

Jen awoke an hour later. The strange dream with Mimi was still with her. Plus, her arm hurt. She looked under the bandage. The scratches were still red.

Mimi's claw marks!

Before she went to the kitchen, she washed her arm with hot water and soap. It stung, but it felt better.

HEALTH TIP
Floss between
all your teeth

When she opened the bathroom door, Mimi was in the hall.

"You're still the worst cat ever," she told her pet.

"Well, so what? You're the worst owner," Mimi shot back.

Wait. What? There was no chance this was a dream. But cats didn't talk. Which meant that she, Jen, must have gone crazy. Maybe it was cat scratch fever without the fever.

She took a breath. "Okay. I'm hearing

you in my head. That doesn't make sense. I don't do that."

Mimi rolled onto her back. She put her paws in the air. "I don't do this," she told Jen. "But does that mean I can't? I think not. I'm doing it now. Anyway, even if I can talk to you? There are lots of words I don't know. Not yet. Rub my belly."

"No."

"Oh, come on, Jen. I know you want to."

Jen did want to rub it. That's what girls did to their cats. So she went to Mimi and rubbed her tummy. For the first time ever, Mimi purred.

"Good," Mimi told her. "A little higher."

"This doesn't make sense," Jen said.

"Now under my chin," Mimi said. "And when you're done, can I go outside?"

Jen swallowed. Everything else was normal. The water had run in the sink. The soap had bubbled.

"I'll be a lot nicer if you let me out," Mimi told her. "I hate to tell you, but this place feels like jail. I need to chase a bird or two. Climb a tree. You know? Do cat stuff."

The house was on one level. There was

other cat stuff

a basement. She and Dawn liked to have sleepovers down there. Jen's bedroom faced the yard.

Without a word, Jen picked up the cat. She took Mimi to her bedroom window.

"If you run away? I won't care," she said.

"Just let me out of here, girl."

Jen opened the window. Mimi jumped to the ledge. "See ya later, gator."

Mimi bounded to the ground. Then she did a happy dance. "Free at last! Yippee!"

Free at last!

Mimi was still dancing. Jen got her phone. She sent a text to Dawn. "U awake?"

"Yup. Wanna shoot hoops later?" Dawn texted.

It made sense Dawn would ask that. She and Jen were on the same basketball team. But Jen did not want to shoot hoops. She wanted to talk about the cat.

"Get over here. My cat is talking to me."

It took a minute for Dawn to text back. "Sorry. Mom patrol. Say again?"

Jen thumbed slowly. "I said my cat is talking to me. Words. A voice in my head. Like that."

"Are u ok?" Dawn wasn't sure what to say. "Don't move. I'm coming over."

4
PROOF

It was an hour later. Dawn had come over. Mimi had just come back inside.

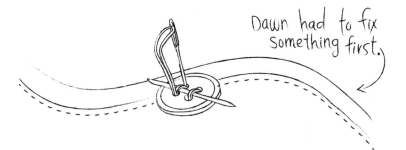

Dawn had to fix something first.

"Thank you for letting me go out," Mimi told Jen.

"You're welcome," Jen said. She and Dawn were on her bed. Mimi lay between them. She was purring again.

"You're talking to the cat again," Dawn said.

Jen shrugged. "She thanked me for letting her go outside. You can't hear her. Right?"

"Duh. No. I can't hear her."

Dawn put her head on Jen's pillow. "You know, Jen. This is hard for me to believe. Cats don't talk. And if they do, girls can't hear them."

"It's the scratches, I think," Mimi told Jen. "They let you hear me."

"That doesn't make sense," Jen replied. "Dawn doesn't hear you."

"Dawn isn't you," Mimi replied.

Jen turned to her. "Mimi said it's from the scratches."

Dawn sat up. "My cat has scratched me. I can't hear a word."

22

"Maybe Mimi is special."

"You know, Jen? You're my friend. Since you are, I want to think this is true. Is there some way to prove it?" Then Dawn snapped her fingers. "I got it."

"What?"

"Leave the room. I'm going to put something under the bed. Only Mimi will see. Then she can tell you what it is. If she tells you, I'll believe you."

Jen stood. The plan made sense. She picked up her cat. Mimi was so nice now. "You got that?"

Mimi mewed. "Totally. It's a piece of mouse."

Jen left the room. Then she closed the door and waited in the hall. Mimi had called it "a piece of mouse." That was funny. It was like a person saying "a piece of cake."

Clown Kitty?

A moment later, the door opened. Mimi and Dawn came out. Dawn closed the door.

"Well?" Jen asked Mimi. "What did she hide?"

Mimi fixed her green eyes on Jen. "Not one thing. A few things. A book. Two pens. Your cell phone. And a big ball. I don't know the word for it."

Jen nodded. "Got it." She looked at Dawn. "Book. Pens. Cell. Basketball."

Dawn gasped, "It's true!"

"Of course it's true," Mimi said to Jen.

"So why can't I hear her?" Dawn whispered.

Mimi rubbed against Jen's right leg. "Don't ask me. I'm just a cat."

They went back into Jen's room. Mimi got up on Jen's bed. The girls joined her. Jen got a brush. For the first time ever, Mimi let herself be brushed.

"See how much happier I am?" Mimi asked. "It's good to have someone to talk to."

Meanwhile, Dawn was jotting some notes on white paper. Jen asked what she was writing.

"Oh, ideas for how to make Mimi useful. We play the Chargers tomorrow in basketball, right?"

"Yep. Two o'clock. Practice today at one. The Chargers practice at five," Jen said.

Dawn got a gleam in her eye. "It would be great to see them practice. We could see how they set up for defense."

Jen shook her head. "Can't do it. All the gym doors are locked."

"Not to cats, they're not," Mimi said.

Jen looked at Mimi. Her cat was right. A person could not spy on a practice. But a talking cat sure could.

5
SWISH!

It was the next day. The game was about to start.

"Okay, guys." Jen looked at the others on her team. "Number 5 only drives to the right. Number 10? Can't stop a bounce pass.

And Number 12? Never boxes out on a foul shot. So it's easy to get the ball."

"How do you know all this?" Cara Page asked. She was the best player on the team.

"We just do," Dawn told her.

"If I didn't know practices were closed, I'd say you spied on them," said Coach Wilson. He turned to the other players. "Go out and play your game. I'm not saying what the girls did is okay. But we'll find out right away if it's true."

"It's true," Dawn promised.

The ref called the teams to the center. The Chargers wore black. The Roses wore white and red. Cara won the tip. She tipped the ball to Dawn. Dawn moved to the basket.

Number 10 was on defense. At the last moment, Dawn pushed a bounce pass to Cara. Number 10 almost fell. Cara made the layup. Two to nothing!

The Chargers came up court. Number 6 got the ball. She started to dribble. She was bad at it. Jen stole the ball. She made a quick pass to Dawn. Dawn took the shot. *Swish!*

It got better from there. At halftime, the Roses had a twenty-point lead. At the end of the game, they had won by thirty. It had been the biggest win of all time.

"I can't wait to tell Mimi!" Jen shouted.

"Who's Mimi?" Cara asked.

"She's …" Jen's voice trailed away. How could she explain?

Psychic Kitty?

Dawn piped up. "A friend. Kind of short. Doesn't eat much. Used to be a jerk. Now she's nice."

Cara looked at them oddly. Then she shook her head. "Good game, you guys."

Jen nodded. It had been a good game. But now that it was over, she felt a little bad. It wasn't like they had cheated to win. But it wasn't like they hadn't cheated either.

6

SPY AGAIN

"It's cheating," Jen said. "I don't want to cheat with Mimi anymore."

"What I'm asking is not for a game. Or a test. So it's not cheating," Dawn said.

"It's still not right," Jen said. Then she looked at Mimi. "What do you think?"

"I think all is fair in love and war," the cat told her. "This is love. I'll do it."

33

"What'd she say?" Dawn asked.

Jen sighed. "Mimi's in."

Dawn jumped happily. "Yes! Mimi, I love you! Good kitty."

It was the next afternoon, Monday. Jen and Dawn had agreed to say nothing about Mimi to anyone. No one would believe Jen's cat could talk. If someone did believe it, that person might steal her.

The girls hated to think that Mimi could be stolen. The best thing to do was to shut up and let her be normal.

Dawn also saw it another way. There was a boy she liked. His name was Jake. He was turning twelve soon. She wanted Mimi to spy on him so she could find out what he liked. Then she would get him a great gift.

"Tell Mimi to look in his window. Try to read his texts," Dawn urged.

"Cats don't read," Jen told her. Again, she turned to Mimi. "Do you know how to read?"

"It's not enough that I can talk?" Mimi said with a loud mew.

Jen shared her words with Dawn.

"Okay. Let's just go over there. She can check out his room," said Dawn. "Maybe there's a band he likes. All I need is one idea."

Taylor → Swift

He secretly loves ❤ girlie pop.

T. S.   1989

Jen looked at her cat again. "You want to do this?"

"Sure. She's your bud. Let's do it," Mimi said.

There was still plenty of light. The two

girls biked over to Jake's house. Mimi rode in a basket on Jen's bike. They stopped about three hundred feet away. Dawn pointed to the house.

Safety first →

"It's that one. His window is the first on the left. Second floor."

"You got that?" Jen asked Mimi.

"Piece of mouse," Mimi told her.

There was a tree outside the window. Mimi ran to it and started to climb. As she did, a chipmunk skipped past her.

Cat genes took over. Mimi went after the chipmunk. The rodent bolted. Mimi gave chase.

"No!" Jen cried. She watched her cat go full speed across the street. A car almost hit her.

"Mimi, stop!"

But the race was on.

7
SCAREDY-CAT

The chipmunk had run up a small tree. Mimi stood at the bottom. She clawed at the bark. That was how Jen and Dawn found her. Jen picked her up.

"What are you doing?" the cat asked.

"Leave the chipmunk alone," Jen said.

"Why? Cats chase them. It's what we're born to do. It's a cat thing."

Chasing is what I do!

"What's she saying?" Dawn asked.

Jen told Dawn.

"Well, she's right," Dawn said. "It's what cats do."

"See?" Mimi told Jen. "Dawn gets it. Even if you don't."

Jen tapped Mimi on the nose. "If you're going to go out with me, no chases. Okay?"

"Okay," the cat agreed. "But if I'm outside

alone, I'll do it. What you don't see won't hurt you."

What you don't see won't hurt you.

"Let's go back to Jake's house," Dawn said. "Mimi still has to do her spying."

Jen didn't want to do that anymore. What just happened with Mimi upset her. She saw how little control she had over this cat. And Mimi was *so* amazing.

One of the houses on Jake's street had a wide swing on a tree by the curb. When they passed it, Jen sat.

"What are you doing?" Dawn asked. "We have work to do."

"We need to talk. Sit with me," Jen said.

Dawn sat. Jen put Mimi on her lap. Each girl petted the cat. Mimi started to purr.

"Don't let the purring fool you," Mimi told Jen. "If this is about me, I'm going to listen."

Jen was quiet for a minute. Then she asked Dawn what she was thinking.

Dawn frowned. "I think I'm sorry. I don't want to take Mimi out like this again. It's too big a risk. She can stay in the yard."

"Thanks for that. But it's more than that. Mimi is a special cat. You know it. I know it. She can do what most cats can't," Jen said.

Mimi spoke up. "Not true! All cats talk. It's just that most humans can't hear us."

Jen told Dawn what Mimi had said.

Dawn sighed. "I guess that's true. You're so lucky to have her."

"I am lucky to have her. But think how great it could be if all kids could learn to talk to their cats." She scratched Mimi's head. "I think we should take her to the state college. They have a vet school. They can study her." She looked down at her cat. "You will be safe there. Don't worry."

Mimi screeched, "No! No, no, no, no, no!"

"No need to tell me what she said. I got it," Dawn told Jen.

Right after that, Mimi got stiff. Her ears perked up. She looked this way and that.

"What's going on?" Jen asked.

Something was wrong. Maybe Mimi smelled a big dog. The cat's tail puffed up.

"Big shake! Big shake! Got to run. Big this way and that way. So big! Must run. Run! Now!"

Jen had no idea what her cat was talking about. Not that it mattered. For a second time in an hour, Mimi bolted.

8
BIG SHAKE

Jen and Dawn looked for Mimi. They got lots of help. Plenty of kids and grown-ups joined in the search. But there was no sign of her. After four hours, they quit. If Mimi didn't come home on her own, Jen said she would put up signs.

It was a school night, but Dawn stayed over. They made signs. They would get up with the sun to look for Mimi and put up the signs.

All night Jen blamed herself for the cat running away. She decided it had not been a dog. It had been her words about the state college. She had upset Mimi.

"She was scared that the vets might hurt her," Jen said. "That had to be why she ran off. I was such an idiot. If I were a cat? I would do the same thing."

She and Dawn were in the basement. Jen's parents said they could stay up till ten. Her parents were going to the movies. They liked to go during the week. It was less crowded. Food was half price.

The girls had a bowl of popcorn near their sleeping bags. Jen wanted some. She wasn't very hungry. But eating would give her something to do.

Dawn pushed the bowl to her. "Mimi's smart," she told Jen. "She'll come back."

"Yeah," Jen said it. But she didn't believe it. "You know what? I'm tired of talking. Let's go to sleep."

"Got your alarm set?"

Jen checked her phone. She nodded. She had set it for five thirty.

They washed up. Then Jen moved for the

light switch. But she never got to it. The room started to shake. Not just a little. A lot. And not just the room. The whole house.

"Earthquake!" Dawn shouted.

"Get in the doorway!" Jen cried.

The girls knew what to do in an earthquake. The safest place was in a doorway. It had good support. But it was hard to get over to it. The room rocked. Stuff on the shelves came down. The big-screen TV crashed to the floor.

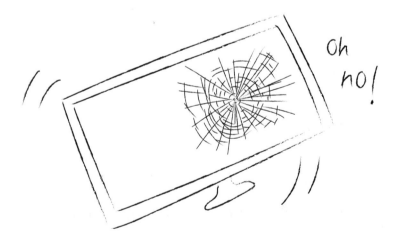

Oh no!

48

Jen had been in a small quake before. But this was no small quake. It was a huge one.

"Big shake! Big shake!" Mimi had said that.

Jen figured it out.

Omigod. Animals can sense when a quake is coming. She was trying to warn us!

The girls made it to the doorway. Then the room went black.

9
TRAPPED

The shaking was all done twenty seconds later. The room stayed black.

Felt like so much longer.

"That was crazy!" Dawn said. "And the power's out."

"I know! You okay?"

"Yeah," Dawn said. "How about you?"

"Yeah. I'm okay. I wish my parents were here," Jen said.

Jen waited for her eyes to adjust to the dark. Her parents had made plans for an earthquake. There were flashlights plugged into a lot of outlets. They came on if the power went out. She spotted one of them across the room. Its light was on.

She pointed. "I'll get it," Jen told Dawn.

"Watch out for broken glass," Dawn warned.

"You're right."

Jen stepped to the light. It came easily out of its holder. She found another light behind her sleeping bag. Now both girls could see.

They shined the lights around the basement. It was wrecked. There was a ton of damage. They were lucky not to be hurt.

"We better go outside," Jen said. "There could be another quake."

"Then let's call our folks," Dawn said.

"What about Mimi?" Jen asked. Then she relaxed. The cat knew the quake was coming. She would be fine.

The stairs were behind them. They got to the top. But the door was jammed shut. No telling what was on the other side. No way could they get out. They were stuck.

Then Jen snapped her fingers. There was one other way. Near the washing machine was a window. It wasn't very big. But she and Dawn were pretty small. They could climb up on the washer. Then they could slip through the window.

Smashed →

She told Dawn her idea. They went to the washer and dryer. It was no problem to get on the washer. The window was above it. But like the door, the window was mostly smashed shut. The gap was just a few inches. There was no way to get out.

"Let's try our phones," Jen told her. She took out her cell. But there was no service.

"No bars," Dawn said.

"Same here. The cell towers are dead."

Dawn was worried. "What do we do now?"

"Your folks know we're here. So do mine. They'll come. We just have to wait."

Then Jen smelled something scary. Gas. The house had gas heat. If the pipe had broken, then gas could spill out. That was what they smelled. It would take only a little spark to ignite it. They had to turn off everything that could spark. Even the lights.

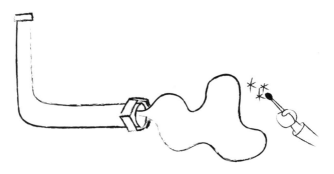

"Um, Jen?"

"Yeah?"

"It smells like gas in here."

Jen nodded. "Yep. We have to turn off the lights and phones. We don't want a fire."

Dawn sighed. "It's worse than that. Gas can choke us. We won't be able to breathe. Where's the shutoff?"

Jen thought hard. "Outside."

"Then pray help comes soon."

Jen nodded. "I will." Jen did pray. If help didn't come, she and Dawn might die.

10
SAVED

"How long has it been?" Dawn asked.

"I don't know. I think two hours. If our cells were on, we would know. But we can't risk a spark. I think it's my turn at the window."

If they were on

For the last few hours, the girls sat on the washing machine. Every few minutes, one of them would get close to the smashed window. That person would call for help and enjoy the fresh air. It was helping them to stay alive.

No one had come to help them. Other people had quake problems too.

There were two really bad things for the girls. The smell of the gas was very strong. Plus, they had no idea at all if help would come. The quake had been huge. Their parents had not come. That had to mean the roads were closed. Or worse. There were sirens. But they were very far away

Then Jen heard an odd sound. The sound of claws on metal.

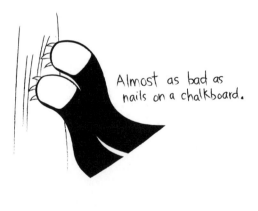

Almost as bad as nails on a chalkboard.

"Hey! You in there? Jen? Jen!"

Jen knew the voice.

"Omigod! It's Mimi!"

"What?" Dawn cried. "Where?"

Jen jumped off the washer. She went to the sound of the claws. It was somewhere under the basement floor. "Mimi? You there?"

Mimi screeched. They both heard it.

Jen snapped her fingers. She got it. There was a crawl space under the house.

"I'm turning on my light," she told Dawn. "Pray there is no spark."

Jen flicked on the light. Whew. No spark. No fire started. She went to a metal plate on the floor. It covered the crawl space. She pulled it open. There was her cat. She shined the light at Mimi. The cat came up into the basement.

"Big shake," Mimi said. "I tried to warn you. I don't know the word for big shake."

"Earthquake," Jen told her.

"Earthquake," the cat repeated. "Then I ran away. Sorry. It's in the genes."

Jen picked up her cat. It was so good to have her in her arms. "I forgive you, Mimi. I love you so much! We need help. We need to get out of here. Wait." She turned to Dawn. "Find paper. And a pen. Write a note. Say we're down here."

HELP! We are stuck down here. Follow the cat to find us... ♡Jen Dawn

Dawn wrote the note. Jen tucked it into Mimi's collar. "Bring it to the people in the red trucks. Then come back. Hurry!"

"Piece of mouse," Mimi said.

"Can we maybe come out with you?" Dawn asked.

"No. Too tight. I'll be back," Mimi said.

Jen nodded. "Mimi says it's too small."

Mimi jumped down into the crawl space.

Jen and Dawn didn't have to wait long. Thirty minutes later, they heard voices. "Hey! Anyone in there?"

Soon the firefighters had cut around the window. Mimi jumped inside to keep the girls company. A few firefighters jumped inside too. They helped the girls out.

"Your cat saved your lives," the lead firefighter said when they were safe. The other firefighters were still coming out of the basement.

Super Kitty?

"She's the best cat ever," Jen said.

"Where is she?" Dawn asked.

"I think she's waiting for my guys," the head firefighter said.

Jen leaned forward. "Come on, Mimi."

Mimi stuck her head out. "There's still two more fire—"

"Watch out!" Dawn yelled.

It happened fast. The house settled. What was left of the window gave way. The top came down onto the bottom. Mimi was right there.

"Mimi!" Jen screamed.

It was too late. The cat was crushed.

The funeral for Mimi was two weeks later. They waited so the firefighters could come. The quake had been bad. Many people had died. Even more lost their homes.

Jen and her family were staying at Dawn's house. Jen's place would need to be rebuilt. But they could still bury Mimi in the backyard. Jen's family was there. So was Dawn's. The firefighters came with a man who played bagpipes.

WEIRDEST looking instrument, but Mimi loved it.

The lead firefighter was the first to talk. "We are here to honor a hero. Mimi gave her life so one of my people could live. If she had not come out when she did, one of my team would have been crushed. Every one of us thanks this cat. Thank you, Mimi. And now, I think Jen has a few words."

Jen got up. She had dug the hole for Mimi. The cat's body was in a box. They had kept her at the vet's until it was time to bury her.

"Mimi was ... a great cat. She wasn't always so great. But she got better as she got older. That's a lesson for all of us. I felt at the end like I could talk to her. And she could talk to me. And then she saved Dawn and me. And a firefighter. I hope all our lives can have so much meaning. I hate to say goodbye to her. But I guess I have to. Goodbye, Mimi."

Jen put the box into the ground. Everyone put a little dirt on it. The piper played. She heard a lot of crying. She cried too. What she'd said was true. She hoped her own life could mean as much as Mimi's life. And she hoped every girl could have a cat as great as Mimi.

Even if that cat didn't talk.